a boy named
AARON

Charleston, SC
www.PalmettoPublishing.com

A Boy Named Aaron
Copyright © 2023 by Tony Torres

All rights reserved

No portion of this book may be reproduced, stored in
a retrieval system, or transmitted in any form by any means—
electronic, mechanical, photocopy, recording, or other—
except for brief quotations in printed reviews,
without prior permission of the author.

Paperback:979-8-8229-1939-6
eBook:979-8-8229-1940-2

a boy named AARON

TONY TORRES

Watching the tiny mushroom dust clouds that formed as the stones hit the ground after having bounced off his filthy and ill-fitting tennis shoes became entertaining for eleven-year-old Aaron, who had just run away from home and was on his way to his uncle Mario's workplace in Ponce, Puerto Rico. Ponce is located on the halfway point of the southern coastline of the island, far from Lajas, where Aaron initiated his journey. He was on his way to ask his uncle to take him in. It was just after midday, and the sun was punishing the earth on the desert-like terrain of the southern coast of the island. Carrying nothing more than a blue denim backpack made by his mother with a half-used composition notebook and an almost new and recently sharpened number 2 pencil to journal, the boy attempted his journey. He had figured that he no longer needed his old textbooks because soon he would receive new ones at his new school so he randomly tossed one at a time from his backpack as he walked. Also, it seemed like a good idea because the load became easier to carry.

Aaron hated his thick black curly hair, which now felt like flames under the heat of the sun. His chubby cheeks glowed red. His big brown eyes looked mostly to the ground, avoiding the harsh sand blown by the wind. Once in a while, squinting, he would raise his sights toward the front to make sure that he was still heading in the right direction. He was also avoiding looking up to the sky to find out why there was not a cloud or bird in it at that particular time.

His fair skin showed that his eleven-year-old body was not used to this climate; after all, it had not been quite two years since his family had moved from New York City. Along with the fair skin, some physical features gave away his African descent, for example his curly black hair, slightly wider nose, and fuller lips.

His school uniform had consisted of a white buttoned-down shirt and navy-blue pants, but by this time, the shirt had changed to a darker shade of cream, and his pants looked gray.

The boy had walked for miles after dropping off his younger brother, Milton, and sister, Maria, at school early that morning before he started his quest. Little

Milton was a year younger and also had curly hair, but it was light brown. He wore black-framed glasses. His sister, Maria, had waist-length straight black hair but wore it in two ponytails, one to the left and one to the right. She had very cute girly features, like small brown eyes, a small perked-up nose, and tiny, naturally red lips. She looked more like their aunt Ann, Uncle Mario's wife.

Aaron did not share his plan with his siblings because he thought that they would not understand and were better off with one less mouth to feed at home. Like every morning, he had led them to the schoolyard, where then they ran freely into the chaotic and noisy multitude of children in search of their classmates and friends before the morning bell. Once the starting class sound was dispatched, he saw Milton and Maria head to their respective classrooms. He then turned around and went out the gate without ever saying a word to a classmate or his siblings. He was leaving it all behind and starting fresh…at eleven years of age.

Although there was rarely a car on the road, he walked well to the side of it because it had become so hot that the asphalt was sticky, and the tar smell sometimes became a bit overwhelming. The boy was determined to reach his destination even if he had to walk all the way there. After all, he had looked at a map of Puerto Rico and had seen that his uncle worked halfway across the island…and the island was not that large. He was also counting on hitchhiking, just like in the movies. One compassionate stranger after another would drive him as close as possible to his uncle's, and he would arrive just before quitting time. But the few cars that did pass by him did not slow down at all. Every so often, a gentle but warm breeze would reenergize him and replace the tar smell with thin but large clouds of dust and sand. Run-down shacks sparsely littered the desert landscape. Some seemed to be inhabited because Aaron could see a full clothesline. Spaced so far apart and weathered, they were almost camouflaged.

His uncle's workplace was a commercial truck repair shop, and he was the lead mechanic. Tough, dark-tanned skin covered his medium but stout build. He was about forty and wore his short, curly salt-and-pepper hair pulled back. He seemed to always wear a smile. He had big, strong, leathery hands that were adorned with abstract art created by the thousands of tiny nicks and burns gifted from his years of working on trucks. Aaron's image of the man was that of a quiet, sweet man who always wore a white T-shirt and blue Dickie work pants. Mario was Bill's older brother. He had taken him in after Bill and his family fled New York because of rising safety concerns. It was the mid-seventies, and New York had become like a scene from a low-budget postapocalyptic crime thriller. The city laid off a lot of people, and the Transit Authority went on strike…Crime ran rampant.

As the boy bent on one knee to tie an undone shoelace, a drop of sweat from his forehead fell onto the front of his shoe, instantly creating a tiny mud puddle that disappeared instantly. Aaron then heard the unmistakable sound of an automobile slowly making its way off the road and stopping just behind him. The crackling sound of the tires rolling over the unpaved surface gave the boy hope that a good Samaritan had come to his rescue to get him closer to his intended destination. While still on one knee tying his shoe, he turned his head and squinted his eyes in an attempt to taper some of the glare away. What he saw was a large black-and-white police patrol car. Having recently come from Brooklyn, New York, he had witnessed police brutality in his former neighborhood and feared for his safety. He turned his head quickly to the left and then right, hoping to see an escape route, but all he saw was a barren desert. Tired and thirsty, he threw his hands in the air just as he had seen people do many times on TV and in the movies when they got arrested.

Laughing, the two policemen stepped out of their patrol car and assured Aaron that he was not in any trouble and they just wanted to help…in Spanish. Both officers were fair-skinned and clean-cut middle-aged men and wore their uniforms to perfection. Both had light-brown hair and eyes, but one looked slightly older than the other and had a larger nose. Aaron was still learning the language but understood perfectly what they meant. He was still a bit on edge until the younger officer handed him a bottle of water. The boy grabbed the plastic bottle and gulped it down in what seemed one swallow. The officers managed to convince the boy to get into the police car by telling him how dangerous it was to be out in that kind of heat. Plus, the car had air-conditioning and more water. He still approached cautiously, holding the empty water bottle like a comfort blanket. Slowly he made his way into the car. The police officer on the passenger side of the front of the police car asked Aaron what he was doing and where was he going as the car made its way onto the pavement.

With naive excitement, Aaron was convinced that the police were there to rescue him so he began to spill his guts freely…in Spanglish, a combination of Spanish and English that was commonly spoken by Puerto Ricans raised in the United States.

"We used to have un apartmento bonito with lots of toys and stuff. We played in the park todo el dia. We would go to zoos and museos and have ice cream!" Changing his facial expression from one of excitement to one of displeasure, he added how his mom and dad had suddenly decided to move to the island and had thrown away almost all their clothes and toys. He commented that they had lived in a storage area beneath his uncle Mario's house but had just recently moved to another house. He also confessed that his parents kept fighting with each other and drank too much.

The officers often looked at each other smiling as they listened to the boy. Having heard similar stories their entire careers, they had no reason to believe that this was any different than any other runaway case.

A few minutes into the drive, while telling his story, Aaron saw the police officer who was driving reach for the radio in the center of the dash. He began speaking into the handheld device. He mentioned that he was coming in with a lost child. The station acknowledged. At that point, Aaron quickly tried to reiterate that he was not lost and that he was on his way to his uncle's place of work. The desperation was becoming clear in the boy's voice and physical agitation. He spoke of his uncle as if he could walk on water. He explained how his serious, leathery face could instantly switch into a day-changing smile and how his kids had everything they wanted as well as a nice big house. He also mentioned that his aunt and uncle brought Cheez Whiz home from the grocery store and that was a luxury afforded only by rich people. With his eyes in full sparkle, he told them how he and his siblings were not allowed to drink milk, but his cousins enjoyed chocolate milk every night before bed. While rubbing his belly, he said he wished he could do the same. He then quickly added that he would be sharing with his siblings as well if he ever had some.

Soon enough, the patrol car veered off the road onto a chain-link-fenced patch of land with a small white square concrete building with another police car parked beside it. It was surprising to see patches of green grass on the pathway as they walked toward the building. A lone small palm tree decorated the center of the front area of the building along with two flag posts, one displaying an American flag and the other the Puerto Rican flag. The structure looked like a tiny white jail cell placed in the middle of the desert as some kind of practical joke. Instead of some fancy tropical or modern facade, above the entrance on a plain concrete slab in crudely painted blue letters were the words "Cuartel de la Policia," which meant "Police Station."

As he stepped into the small building, he felt the alleviating sensation of the air-conditioning running at full power. His hair waved with the blowing of the appliance. He was quickly asked to take a seat on a large wooden chair next to a water fountain near the entrance. An extremely long wooden table with an almost hidden sliding door on the far right-hand side stood dividing the building in half. The center of the table was shaped like a combination of a desk and a podium. When the officers approached the shoulder-height structure, the officer on the other side moved his large wooden chair to make himself more visible to the officers and listen.

The officer at the desk had great view of the row of empty jail cells beside him and the front entrance. He wore a perfectly detailed uniform as well but had a huge beer belly that would cause alarm in most people. Thick gray eyebrows and no facial hair made the calm officer look righteous and confident. By the way he used his hands to rub his eyes, it did not take a rocket scientist to know that this man had been napping nicely before he was interrupted. The walls, bars, and cells on that side of the building were light greenish in color and did not seem to have aged well. The paint on the walls showed peeling, cracks, and concrete patchwork that was never painted over. The place on the cell door where a prisoner's hands would be as he begged for mercy was completely stripped of paint and glinted with raw steel. On the wall by the door was a map of Puerto Rico with the road he had been on highlighted and a pin indicating the station's position. Wondering what could've gone wrong, he noticed that he was nowhere near his destination, though he had walked for hours.

He did not clearly understand the full extent of the conversation because he could barely hear over the sound of the air-conditioning unit and it was also completely in Spanish, but Aaron could sense that they were not taking him to his uncle's workplace but back home. All three officers seemed very engaged in a discussion of what to do. They would be talking, suddenly pause, look at him, and then continue talking. They did this several times. The boy desperately began to search for ways he could escape from the building and continue his journey, but it was quickly obvious that there was no place to run. There was only desert outside and no cover.

After a few moments, the officers turned back to Aaron. The younger one crouched to his eye level and explained that his mother and father were very worried about him and that it was very dangerous to be out alone in the street. The boy's heart dropped, and he began to cry. Nonetheless he put his head down and calmly walked back out of the building and got into the patrol car escorted by the officers. Having already gotten his home address, they proceeded to drive there in silence. The sound of the patrol car's engine roared down the empty road as if it too was trying to escape the hot asphalt. It was occasionally interrupted by the gibberish that came from the officer's radio and the young boy's sobbing. In tears, he tried convincing them that he would get beaten if he was taken back, but they kept silent and looked straight ahead. The boy cried himself to sleep.

It was just starting to get dark when Aaron awoke and sat up as the patrol unit slowed onto the sidewalk curb in front of the house located on the main street almost in the center of the town. With the charisma and stance of an evil queen from some Disney animation film, with her arms crossed, a tall, black-haired woman wearing a long velvety purple robe stood there. By the obvious similarities to the boy, such as fair skin and mild African descent features like a slightly wider nose and thicker lips, they could see this was his mother, Dana. Surrounded by three other neighborhood mothers, visibly angry and worried, the mother made eye contact with her son as the patrol car came to a halt in front of them at the house. His eyes widened when he saw the anger in her eyes and how she clenched her fist. His little heart began to pound harder like some sort of out-of-control African percussion competition was taking place in the center of his chest.

Like a couple of handsomely paid street snitches, the officers informed Dana of where and how they had found Aaron, as well as why he claimed he had run away. As the officers spoke, Dana guided Aaron toward her side and tightly secured the back of his shirt with a clenched fist, ensuring that he could not run from her side. The officers did not notice this because they were too focused on their conversation. After their brief explanation, the officers asked Dana to please not beat the kid because he really didn't understand the implications of his actions and added that he was not the first and would not be the last boy to try to run away. Dana only nodded in agreement and with a smirk, waved as the police officers drove away.

The sarcastic smirk on her face clearly indicated to Aaron that she was going to do whatever she felt was necessary to discipline her own child and not what the police or anyone would suggest. She continued waving the officers goodbye as she watched the patrol cars shrink down the narrow street.

Feeling betrayed by the men who were supposed to protect him, the boy was suddenly violently shoved through the front door and into the small living room, where he fell to the ground. Hearing the commotion, his siblings quickly came out of their rooms. All bedrooms surrounded the living room in the small house. Screaming at the top of her lungs, Dana menaced the boy with words like, "You want to run away? You want to run away? I will teach you how to run away!" She then snapped the electric cord off the iron she had been using to get her nightshift clothes ready with a single pull and headed toward the terrified and crying boy. Looking up from the floor, he raised his little hands as if to protect himself from the lashings he was about to receive.

"Please, Mommy, don't hit me. I won't leave again, I promise!" Aaron cried in inconceivable fear.

She then told him to get naked and kneel by the door that gave way from the living room to the side of the house. He kept screaming for his mother not to beat him as he then knelt by the door, trying to cover as much of his body as quickly as he could to protect himself.

She grabbed the eleven-year-old by the hair with one hand and pulled him from facing the door. She began to strike him with the electric cord wherever she could land a lash. He kept trying to cover himself, but she was faster and much stronger than he was. Out the corner of his eyes, he could see Milton and Maria watching in horror as tears of fear came from their innocent little eyes. With every lash, Dana asked Aaron if he still wanted to leave. The boy's body would twitch violently with each lash. With one hand, she would lift him up from the floor by his curly hair or wherever she could get a hold of him and lash with the other. Then things changed drastically. The boy looked up to his mother, and what he saw was an avatar of a gigantic white shark with its giant black eyes rolled back, heading toward him. He now began to scream for help from anybody. It was at this time that his mother in a state of blind anger wrapped the cord around his neck and began to tighten furiously to keep him from moving and screaming.

Aaron's cries for help changed to cries, pleading for his mother not to kill him. She kept tightening the cord around the boy's neck while screaming, "I'm going to kill you! I'm going to kill you! I'm going to kill you!" Completely exhausted from trying to fight off the attack, Aaron could hardly breathe or move. Soon enough, he gave up fighting. His body could not resist anymore and went limp. In his peripheral vision, he saw his siblings shaking and crying and lamented their suffering due to his trespass. But just as he was ready to pass out, his mother's younger sister, Eleanor, who was there on a summer trip from New York ran toward them and with a hard shove, she was able to separate Dana from the child. They argued about the severity of the punishment handed out and who was right on how to raise this child specifically. Eleanor pointed to where the child lay and mentioned the scars and blood on the child. Dana then grabbed Aaron by lifting him by the hair and dragged him through the narrow hallway and into the bathroom. She then turned the cold shower on and shoved him under the water. Aaron wept as quietly as he could when he began to see the welts on his arms, sides, and legs. The blood and water blended as it ran down his legs onto the shower floor and then into the drain. The cold water felt like ice pellets on his shivering body, but it was better than getting lashed, he thought to himself.

After few minutes, she pulled him out of the shower and shoved him into his bedroom. She made him lie face down and proceeded to cover him with some thick ointment. But as he slowly passed the living room like a condemned prisoner, he saw his aunt Eleanor with a small pail and a few bloody rags scrubbing the floor.

At one point during the night, Dana opened the door slowly, and all Aaron could see was her dark silhouette as she whispered, "You think that's bad. Wait till your father comes home." Then she slowly closed the door again. The fatalistic message only made the boy care less about his own life now. He felt that he preferred death to another beating like this one.

Working nightshift at an electronic components factory, Bill, Aaron's father, was a very strict man who usually left the correction policies to Dana but would not shy from dealing his own punishments sometimes after the fact. Tall, thin, and with what some called at the time a porn-star mustache, Bill was a very good-looking middle-aged man. He had a full head of straight jet-black hair, just like his father before him. He was also known as a ladies' man and counted with a hoard of drinking buddies.

When Aaron heard his father walk into the home, he began to tremble, not knowing what to expect. He heard his mother proudly justifying the beating and encouraging Bill to hand Aaron the final lesson for wanting to run away. The boy began to tremble in terror as he heard the angry footsteps heading toward his door. Bill busted the child's bedroom door like a hardcore and trigger-happy policeman on a raid and turned the light on. He was ready to lash out at the boy but was not ready for what he saw. He saw his eleven-year-old son lying face down, naked with a number of welts covering a good portion of his back, legs, and arms. Aaron noticed the shock and horror on his father's face as he looked down on him. His eyes opened wide, surveying the child's body, and his mouth slightly opened, expressing his emotion. Without a single word to the child, the father turned away and closed the door hastily behind him. An argument ensued with Bill calling Dana an animal. Aunt Eleanor gave her account of the incident while adding that she could no longer stay in that home. They argued for what seemed like hours as Aaron drifted to sleep.

Beams of sunlight came through the sides of the aluminum storm windows early in the morning, like gentle alarm clock from nature. Aaron got out of bed and tried to put on his clothes to get ready for school. He heard the normal sounds and smells coming from the dining room, where his mother and siblings had gathered and were having breakfast. Aunt Eleanor was no longer with them. The only person he felt had defended him and saved his life had left during the night and did not even say goodbye. He was only able to put his underwear on because the welts hurt too much as he tried to put on his pants. The polyester rubbed over the injuries, making them feel raw all over again. The white short-sleeved uniform shirt stuck to his back because of the still-clotting blood, so he took it off. On it, he saw three bright-red stripes of blood. His mother came into the room and told him that he was not going to school but instead was to stay home for a few days. Dana gave no explanation, but the reason was now obvious. Milton and Maria stopped in mid-conversation, and with shock visible in their eyes, they looked at their older brother from his bedroom door. Their mother rushed the two children away from the room and out the front door where they met a small group of neighborhood children walking their way to school.

For the next week, he was lathered in ointment and confined to his room—no TV, no talking, eating alone in the bedroom, and using the bathroom was to be on a permission basis only. He spent his time during the day journaling and daydreaming that somebody loved him or cared. Although surrounded by family, he now felt isolated and shunned because of his intention to run away. Then at night again, he would whisper for God to either kill him or restart his life to the moment he decided to run away as he gazed into the star-littered sky. The sense of wanting to belong made him wish that he were one of the stars decorating the quiet peace through the night.

A full week had passed, and the markings on the boy's body were healed enough that he could bathe and dress on his own. Tentatively he approached the side door, the site of his beating, to make his way to the backyard to play. Like a horror movie trailer, he experienced flashbacks of the beating and could hear the loud screams. But as quickly as they came, they left. For a brief moment, in fear, he paused on his way. Then he regained enough of his childish and naive courage to continue walking. Anxiety was beginning to take root in his heart as his hand reached for the doorknob and turned it slowly. As the door opened and invited daylight in, he squinted and noticed that on the other side of the door by the horizontal narrow concrete path and fence the gossip-spreading silver-haired granny next door was staring at him. That side entrance was only about ten feet directly across from the neighbor's house. Aaron saw the elderly lady looking right at him from her kitchen window and quickly make the sign of the cross as he stepped out the door and onto the concrete walkway. As a child, Aaron found the woman's gesture somewhat odd and did not understand.

Before he ran down the steps and into the yard to play, he noticed how close both neighbors' houses were to his home. He wondered what they had heard during his beating. They must have heard his cries for help and his mother's yelling as she branded him with the cord from the iron.

Monday came, and Aaron walked to school with his siblings just as they routinely had prior to the runaway incident. Dana had sent a note to the school staff with Aaron stating that he had been involved in a yard work accident and had needed to recover. She assured them that all was fine now. All seemed normal for everyone else except for Aaron. His eyes now saw a different point of view than the rest of the children's, he believed. While the chaotic sounds of children at play blended together, he seemed oblivious to it for the first time, and it made him feel uncomfortable. The now excess noise and visual stimulation raised his anxiety levels. This had never happened before. He saw groups of children playing together innocently while others engaged in masculine horseplay games and felt that he no longer belonged among them. He felt different.

During recess, he stayed inside the classroom, alone, journaling. He wrote of how lonely he felt and would ask himself in the writings why no one cared about him. None of the adults at school or at the grocery store mentioned the healing but still visible scars on his young body. Only one fellow student who was a close neighbor commented indifferently that his whole family had heard the screams down the block, and his father had commented, "He must've done something really bad to deserve a beating like that." This confirmed to Aaron that the beating and its severity had been justified…It seemed the norm to everyone he encountered.

Tonka trucks and GI Joes quickly became a thing of the past. The days of playing alongside his siblings came to an abrupt halt. No more playing with Hot Wheels cars and making believe that he was the top artist on the radio. Aaron now felt that in order to not invite another beating, he would have to try his best to be an adult. This way, his parents would favor and treat him as an equal human being.

At night, Aaron would stare out his bedroom window and into the starry sky, teary-eyed, and ask God to please kill him. He felt that he had been deceived and betrayed by all those he thought were supposed to care for and protect him. The police had turned him in without questioning really anything or considering his fatalistic pleading. The school staff had made no comment and asked no questions about the wounds or the missing week of class. Most adults in the family did not comment either. There were a couple who said with a smile, "Bet you won't try to run away again." He wondered if it would have been any other member of the family getting beaten like that, would they have allowed this to happen? He was convincing himself that he had truly dishonored his parents and so deserved what he got and that was the reason no one came to his aid—it was justified.

Days seemed to move at a faster pace, and routine chores from home and school became stressful. It was difficult to focus on anything because his mind kept reminding him that he was less than most of the population. Many times, he could feel the new addition to his already stressful life creeping up: crying spells. Often now, he would find himself frantically searching for a secluded and soundproof place to hide and release his overwhelming buildup of emotions. Like a fatally injured lion roaring fearlessly to cover his inevitable fate, he held nothing back in his cry.

Nights were no better, as the faces of those who knew then and by now about the beating flew through his head with smiles. He saw them all as expert deceivers and hypocrites. Authority had revealed itself as nothing more than a disguised oppression designed to keep the good and innocent people under control. The only people he felt that he could trust were his siblings, Milton and Maria, but they were too young to help in any fashion; plus, they too were under the oppressive anvil of his parents.

Creative new plans to escape the household frequently crossed Aaron's eleven-year-old mind, but the painful memory of the beating would play a major role in their own demise. There were times when he drew out plans with time tables and distances and then, in anger and frustration, tore the page out of his composition notebook, crushed it, and then tossed it onto the floor while resisting the crying spells. The root of his frustration was that if he was able to escape successfully, he still had no place to go. His uncle Mario knew of the incident and had made no comment…Obviously, he did not care, Aaron thought. The police would only try to deceive him and take him back to his parents, resetting the table for further trauma. The school staff was too focused on the constant fundraising and had previously demonstrated that he was not important.

Like many so-called religious people, his parents would send their children to church, as they had free time to do whatever they wanted to do while the children were technically being babysat by the clergy. The parents did attend the holiday church services to keep up with appearances, proving the hypocrisy of the adults as far as Aaron was concerned. But religion was very confusing to the boy because the Good Book said that they should not display idols, yet the church was covered in them. The book also said that God loved you more than you could ever imagine and for eternity, but he had hell if you didn't follow all of his impossible rules. It was easy to see all the money that the church was bringing in with every service from the overflowing baskets that the ushers would pass for collection and then deposit into a special receptacle. The people were indoctrinated that the money was to help the poor, yet after every service, there would be a handful of beggars just outside the doors…homeless, hungry, and there. He would see a few people give, but others would completely ignore them or try to shoo them away. Aaron never saw or heard of a food pantry or shelter for these people. They were being ignored by the same people who claimed that they wanted to help, and that kind of resonated with the boy.

When he would question his parents about these issues, he would be smacked across the mouth because he was defaming the church. He asked other adults about his concerns, and he was constantly told to either shut the hell up or assured that he would never understand. All the impossible rules to follow and the constant lessons teaching how you were not and would never be enough in the eyes of God began to not sit so well with Aaron. To the young boy, church was another oppressive state that kept you comfy while they took your hard-earned money, claiming to pay for things that never took place. He thought that perhaps God should have intervened but obviously did not care.

Some afternoons, Aaron would ride a cousin's bicycle to the beach that was about two or three miles from their home to sit alone under a palm tree and journal. The slow crashing of the waves and the breeze that flew through the palm trees' musical leaves were a great melodic background theme for his writing. The aromatic peek-a-boo from the meals that some families scattered around the beach would bring to picnic made the boy smile, imagining that he was part of the gathering, but it all would quickly morph into just hunger. He could hear the children laughing as they played in the sand. Every so often, one would call for his mother to show her some monstrosity of a sand sculpture, and she would reply with encouraging and nurturing words. In a way, he envied that interaction. He knew that he could never have that relationship with Dana. He feared her.

On Mother's Day, the year after the beating, Aaron and his siblings executed a childishly planned celebration for Dana. Milton and Maria helped make the house spotless, and Aaron baked a heart-shaped cake with a pan his mother had borrowed from a neighbor and never returned. The kids signed a beautiful Mother's Day card they had made with leftover cardboard from a school project, crayons, and dry flowers. Inside that card was a drawing of a stick family consisting of the mother, father, and three children all holding hands with a mountain and an enormous yellow sun behind it. A little house with a Puerto Rican flag was also included.

Aaron had made a special card of his own and handed it to his mother while they all were enjoying a slice of the cake. Dana glossed over the card, tossed it on the table, thanked Aaron, and continued to eat. The card had only one big red heart on the front. Inside the card were only nine words, "Thank you for letting me live. Your Son, Aaron." He did not give it to her as a sarcastic gift but rather a solemn but grateful one… He wanted her to understand that he did not want her to try to kill him again. This was to be proof of his submissiveness to her. He gave her the same kind of card every year for the next five, and neither ever spoke about the inscription.

For the first time in his life, Aaron wanted nothing for Christmas. After all, they were poor. His birthday gift was forty-five cents, but he could not even purchase a can of soda to celebrate because it costed fifty cents. He did want his siblings to get stuff, and they did… underwear. Meanwhile, holiday movies marathoned on TV flaunted the celebrations and gatherings of the well-to-do all season long. Some movies attempted to portray what a "real" unfortunate family would supposedly go through, and then some religious miracle would save the season…It was all fantasy. He never heard of anything like that happening to anyone anywhere…only in the movies. Reality was that the rich got richer by not allowing the poor to reach a stage where they would have to share the money pie. Then the poor would submissively accept their fate and be content about it like a corralled flock of blind sheep, and that was becoming unacceptable to him. He kept finding faults in everything and everyone and vowed to someday save the rest of the children in the world from evil.

Something that truly confused Aaron was that while living in New York, he and some of his friends would get bullied because they were supposedly not American despite having been born in New York and their parents being natural-born citizens as well. As Puerto Ricans, they were called names like *spic*, *wetback*, and *banana boat captain.* Yet in Puerto Rico, he and his siblings were bullied because they were American or "Nuyorican" and therefore not Puerto Rican. It seemed that the general consensus among the students was that anyone foreign was there only to try to exploit or intimidate them, and they were going to be preemptive about it.

One day, a bully accompanied by two other juvenile thugs approached Aaron as he was journaling alone under a tree in the far end of the schoolyard. He had not noticed the approaching confrontation, as he was completely focused on writing a rant about how unfair life was and how he would do something about it one day. Angrily he was scribbling his words onto the paper when the bully slapped his notebook from his hands and began to laugh annoyingly loud. The two half-wit-looking thugs joined in on the laughter. In a fit of blind rage, Aaron stood up quickly and began to cover the bully's body with fists as fast and as hard as he could. When he saw the bully go down, he fixed his eyes on the two thugs. They saw a look in his eyes that they had never seen and appropriately took a few steps back. Then they ran away, leaving their bully friend behind.

On the ground, looking up at Aaron, the bully pleaded for peace. Aaron stretched his hand out and helped the bully up. He warned him that it would be much worse if he tried that again. The bully agreed to the boy's conditions and began to walk away when Aaron grabbed him by the back of his shirt and moved him closer to orate his final threat: "I don't want you fucking conmigo or my brother and sister anymore. You are going to stop or yo the paro. You will bully no one else from here on, ever. If I ever legal a saber that you beat someone up, I will beat you up." He then let go of the bully's shirt and pushed him away. The bully left with his head bowed down. Aaron thought to himself that he had scored a major victory, but something inside made him wonder if he now had become the bully.

Now fourteen years old, Aaron was a very sensitive and angry young man. Still in Puerto Rico but in the northeastern part of the island at a town called Isabela, Aaron began his high schooling in a new school. In spite of being an angry teen, he was a reader and enjoyed different genres with the exception of fiction, which he thought was silly and served no purpose. He had good grades. He had already skipped a grade in middle school.

He would later be skipped another grade, but during his first week in school, he actively hunted for the school bully by directly asking some students and by observing the behavior of the physically larger students. He focused on the larger students because he thought that they would try to intimidate the smaller and nonathletic students. It did not take long for the name Carlos to come up several times. The alleged bully was a school team baseball player and traveled around school with a small entourage composed of other jocks. Aaron never saw Carlos actually do any bullying, but the stories, his demeanor, and his attitude were enough for him to make judgment.

Behind the campus's main building, Carlos sat with his entourage and a group of girls. They all sat on a concrete bench that stretched the entirety of the building; it was more like a bottom ledge that the students could sit on. They laughed and giggled while making inappropriate comments to students passing by. Aaron saw this and went to a student who had been physically bullied by Carlos and asked him to identify him in order for there to be no mistake on who would receive judgment. The scared boy walked beside Aaron and pointed out the bully. With purpose, Aaron marched toward Carlos and stood about three feet in front of him. Carlos was significantly larger than Aaron, and he was confused about why this puny subject would walk toward him as if to challenge him. He also sat with an entourage and a group of girls to establish his juvenile dominance. But these things meant nothing to the pumped-up and angry young boy. He started to accuse him of bullying and pointed out some of his victims as a crowd began to gather upon hearing the commotion. He told the bully that no longer would his behavior be tolerated. Carlos tried to avoid confrontation by telling Aaron that he was sorry about his past childish behavior, but Aaron was having none of it and challenged the athlete to a fight.

"Sorry doesn't cut it, maricon. If you brake a plate and say sorry to it, it doesn't fix the fucking plate no matter cuantas veces you say sorry to it. These kids are broken because of you, and they can never be repaired, and so now I will break you." He then proceeded to take his shirt off.

Carlos insisted over and over that he was sorry and did not want to fight Aaron. The anger built up inside the boy increased to such a point that suddenly all became quiet, and in slow motion, he could see Carlo's face contorting as he spoke. He heard Carlos plead in vain and offer excuses to pacify him and be a hero in front of his friends. Without further warning, he began to strike Carlos in the face with a blind fury.

School staff that were in the area ran toward the agitated crowd. Some teachers in the building across from them saw the fight and also ran to stop the mayhem. Carlos never struck Aaron; he only kept trying to block the wild and aimless barrage of fists coming toward him. A couple of the teachers received a few unintended strikes as they separated the boys. While Carlos had some scratches and bruises, his clothing looked like he had been attacked by some large cat. He explained to the teachers how Aaron had come hellbent on a mission to fight him, and he wasn't really sure why. Meanwhile another teacher restrained Aaron from behind because he was still very angry and trying to break himself loose to continue passing judgment on the bully. He was released when he calmed down. Suddenly a large group of kids cheered Aaron, and the teachers noted that.

When Aaron arrived to the front of the principal's office, Carlos had already arrived and was inside. The teacher escort asked him to sit on an old folding chair on the opposite side of the door but across the hallway and wait for his turn. Then the teacher asked the curious student mob to scatter. Some yelled his name out loud as they left the premises. He was beginning to feel that perhaps he was indeed a hero in his own way. The kids cheered his violent action, confirming to the boy that violence could be acceptable. He began to hold his head a bit higher as an involuntary sign of newly found confidence. Again, the beating he received for running away came flashing back through his mind like a horror movie in 3-D on a super large screen. He accepted his beating as absolutely justified but felt deep in his heart that he would never want to know of any other children getting treated that way. There had to be a better way to discipline a child. Aaron also believed that there was no way that the principal was going to understand his reasoning because as another authority figure, he was there only to punish him.

The sound of the principal's office door echoed throughout the school hallway abruptly awakening

Aaron from his thoughts. As Carlos walked out, the two boys made eye contact. Aaron looked upon Carlos with his facial features demonstrating only disgust. Carlos still looked at him confused as he was escorted outside to the hallway.

From inside the principal's office, an angry old man's voice called out his name in perfect Spanish. He stood straight up and then made his way into the school's sentencing room. Principal Ortiz was an older but very well-dressed gentleman. He was sixty years old but looked more like seventy. He had completely slicked back silver hair and a very dark-tanned skin tone. The room was full of boxes of files and cigar smoke. The only open spot was on the chair directly across the principal's desk from him. Pulling the huge and lit cigar out of his mouth, the principal pointed to the chair, looking directly at Aaron. The boy then sat in complete silence, awaiting his sentence. The principal began his lecture in a surprisingly passive tone. He confessed how disappointed he was, knowing what a good student Aaron truly was and that he was wasting his time on nonsense. He also mentioned that the staff had been reviewing his prior school's file and were considering watching him to potentially have him skip another grade, but his actions had demonstrated complete immaturity. It was unacceptable behavior and could get him arrested and thrown in jail.

After the principal spoke his piece, he asked Aaron if he had anything to say for himself. Aaron looked the older man directly in his tired brown eyes and for a moment thought that he could trust him but instantly remembered how in the past police officers had lured him into their vehicle and then taken him to his home to get a beating he would never forget.

The boy bowed his head and told the principal that he was truly sorry about the incident only to avoid a further lecture and get his sentence out of the way as discreetly and as soon as possible so his parents would not find out. But the principal had a lot more to say. He sat back in his chair and began to speak in perfect English but with a heavy Puerto Rican accent and a much firmer tone.

"You know what, kid? I think you are full of shit. You want to play Batman? Go to the fucking movie studios and play that shit there, not in my school. I think that your apology is also full of shit...You don't look sorry to me. You look like you think that I am some stupid motherfucker that you can just lie to and carry on your merry way because of your grades, but let me tell you something, Batman, I have sent little fuckers just like you straight to prison from that very chair you are sitting on. How well do you think that it will turn out in a correctional facility when they find out how you were playing Batman and wanted to fight everybody? If you have anger issues and want to fight, I am sure that you can find a fight every day until the day you die in there, which won't take long once you start fighting everyone."

Aaron looked at the principal and was opening his mouth to attempt to explain his justified position and therefore his actions, but before he could utter a sound, the principal rose from his chair and continued his lecture.

"I may regret this, but for some reason, I get the feeling that you are a good boy—full of shit but a good boy. Do not waste your time and energy fighting; it is not for you. Even boxers hate fighting after a while… and they get paid for it and you don't. If you promise me that you will keep up your grades and not fight anymore, I will make sure that you get skipped another grade and in your senior year will help you find a good college. Now get the fuck out of my office. I'm busy, and shut the door behind you."

The boy replied with a quick "Yes, sir" and rushed out of the office and into the hallway where the escorting teacher waited, standing very serious and tall like a real jailer ready to escort him to his cell. He was then escorted back into the schoolyard.

Keeping their promise to each other, Aaron focused most his energy on his studies, and Principal Ortiz skipped him a grade halfway through his sophomore year and into his junior year. That was when Aaron's parents moved again, having him change schools one more time. It would hopefully be the last time because it was his senior year, he thought. By this time, Milton had transformed into a lean and mean young boy, learning and feeding off his brother's actions because Aaron had not stopped fighting; he just fought outside school property. He went as far as secretly getting a tattoo of a gargoyle on his right shoulder to symbolize his oath of protection to the other vulnerable and weak children.

As his final year in high school was coming to an end, he would hear classmates discussing colleges and careers. He heard how pretty much everyone was receiving college acceptance letters, yet he had not even received or been offered an application of any kind. No one spoke to him about scholarships or grants for college tuition, and when he asked his father about the possibility of going to college, his father dismissed him by telling him that it was best if he just looked for a job because they could not afford college for him.

The crying spells that he had become so masterful in managing were coming back with a vengeance. Every instance he felt that he had been hurt or betrayed flashed before him with more frequency and just as vividly and painfully as ever. Once again, he began to implore God to please kill him in his sleep to end this forsaken sentence. There were no longer future plans because they were for college, and they vanished the day they relocated at the beginning of his senior year. A heavy weight fell upon him as talks of his parents divorcing seemed to be becoming a reality. Bill threatened Dana by telling her that he was leaving almost every day, and if he did, that meant that Aaron would stay behind with his siblings and Dana. He could not understand how only a year prior he had been a popular kid in school and was well on his way to college and freedom, yet today he sat with the prospect of staying home and begging for factory work to help support his brother and sister. Worst of all, he had to do this under Dana's sole rule.

While reading a car magazine at the school library, Aaron saw an army recruitment advertisement. In the add, they promised free room and board along with a fully paid college education at the fulfillment of the contract. Many of his relatives were currently or had been in the military. The more he read, the better the idea looked. He could help support his siblings and travel the world while doing so. Then he could come home and go to college. He had it all figured out in five minutes. He also remembered that he had seen a military recruiting office in the school right by the principal's office.

Early the next morning, Aaron went to the recruiting office at school and was briefed on his options by the sharply dressed army sergeant. Because of his age, he needed his parents' signatures. He knew that his parents would not care as long as he stayed out of their way, and he was correct because when the recruiter came to try to convince his parents they were in the middle of a heated argument and signed the papers without really listening to what the recruiter had to say. That week, Aaron submitted to a battery of written and physical tests to see his fitness worthiness to join the army. It was less than thirty days later when he was informed by his recruiter that he had been accepted and was to leave within the next thirty days if he accepted the offer. With no further talk, he signed the military contract.

Those thirty days seemed to last an eternity. He had promised Milton that he would buy him the latest Kiss CD as soon as he could and promised his Maria whatever she wanted when he returned after basic training. He assured Dana that he would send a check every month to help with the household, and for the first time, he saw a sort of sad look in her eyes when she thanked him.

On the scheduled departing day, he was to meet the recruiter outside his front door with nothing but a few clothing and personal hygiene items at four o'clock in the morning.

Three o'clock displayed on the falling-apart plastic living room wall clock. Aaron had stayed sitting on the couch ready to go since midnight. He then got up slowly, and trying not to make noise, he made his way through the dark house and into the room he shared with Milton. He saw his brother in a peaceful sleep, and in a whisper, he promised him that he would be back for him soon. He gently kissed his forehead and then made his way to Maria's room. He was surprised to see her in bed but with her tiny eyes open and looking at him as he approached her. He asked her why she was not asleep, and she just shrugged her tiny shoulders as if indicating that she did not know why, but then she told him that she was going to miss him. Aaron hugged his sister and kissed her too on the forehead before making the same promise he had made to Milton. Maria nodded her head in agreement and then closed her eyes.

At this time, the boy was unsure if he should enter his parents' bedroom or just leave. When he came to their bedroom door, he found that it was locked so he gently knocked on the door. He heard Bill respond in an almost unintelligible voice, "*What?*"

"I'm leaving," Aaron said in a normal tone of voice.

"OK, be careful."

As Aaron finally stepped out of his home and onto the sidewalk, he went into a crying spell. All the childhood memories flashed incoherently through his mind, but he was able to control it as he clutched a homemade blue denim backpack that his mother had made for him years ago. Inside the bag, he had two of his three pairs of underwear, two of this three white T-shirts, two pairs of socks, and a toothbrush. On an index card, he had the current home address, which more than likely would change very soon, and no phone number…for anyone.

The recruiter arrived right on time. The boy got into the car, finally feeling free yet regretful because he was leaving Milton and Maria behind. He thought of that all the way to the airport.

About the Author

Tony Torres was born in NYC August 1965. His main goal in life is to make the world a better place. Tony is a disabled Army veteran and has two younger siblings; a brother and a sister.

Tony currently resides in West Virginia with his wife Amy and dog Gemma. Tony has three children who are all adults and live in different places. Apart from writing, his hobbies consist of cooking for his family and neighbors and learning from his favorite influential people (like Bruce Lee, Marcus Aurelius, Roberto Clemente, and Jordan Peterson).

You can keep up with his life and blog at www.iamtonytorres.com.

www.ingramcontent.com/pod-product-compliance
Lightning Source LLC
LaVergne TN
LVHW041557070526
838199LV00046B/2024